D0607246

This cat feels
my pain. →

Zeke Meeks is published by
Picture Window Books
A Capstone Imprint
1710 Roe Crest Drive
North Mankato, MN 56003
www.capstoneyoungreaders.com

Library of Congress Cataloging in Publication Data

Green, D. L. (Debra L.)
  Zeke Meeks vs the super stressful talent show / by D. L. Green; illustrated by Josh Alves.
    p. cm. — (Zeke Meeks)
  Summary: Zeke's class is having a talent show, and Brassy Glass, from America's Next
Superstar, will be coming to the show as the judge — but Zeke cannot figure out what
talent he actually has and, as usual, his sisters are no help at all.
  ISBN 978-1-4048-8106-8 (hard cover)
  1. Talent shows—Juvenile fiction. 2. Middle-born children—Juvenile fiction. 3. Brothers and
sisters—Juvenile fiction. 4. Elementary schools—Juvenile fiction. [1. Talent shows—Fiction. 2.
Middle-born children—Fiction. 3. Brothers and sisters—Fiction. 4. Elementary schools—Fiction.
5. Schools—Fiction. 6. Humorous stories.] I. Alves, Josh, ill. II. Title. III. Title: Zeke Meeks
versus the super stressful talent show. IV. Series: Green, D. L. (Debra L.) Zeke Meeks.
  PZ7.G81926Zim 2013
  813.6—dc23   2012028193

Vector Credits: Shutterstock
Book design by K. Fraser

Printed in the United States of America in Stevens Point, Wisconsin.
092012   006937WZS13

Waggles and I →
brainstorming our
talent show act.

Zeke Meeks
vs THE SUPER STRESSFUL TALENT SHOW

BY D. L. GREEN

ILLUSTRATED BY JOSH ALVES

PICTURE WINDOW BOOKS
a capstone imprint

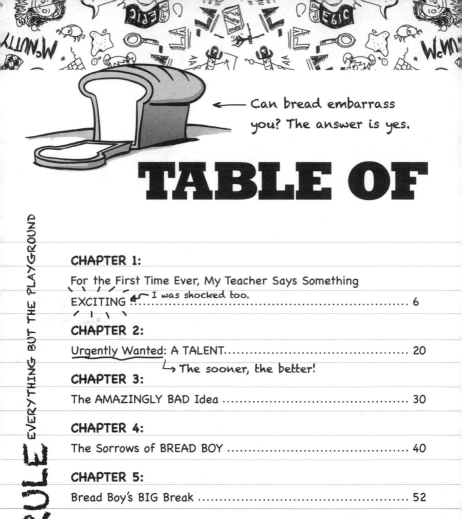

← Can bread embarrass you? The answer is yes.

TABLE OF

CONTENTS

Can you handle our
awesomeness?

→ Do people even wear suspenders anymore?

Definitely comparable to
Grace Chang's fingernails

It's not as easy to do
as you might think!

FINDING YOUR TALENT

GIRLS DROOL

ALL BUT GRACE — SHE BITES

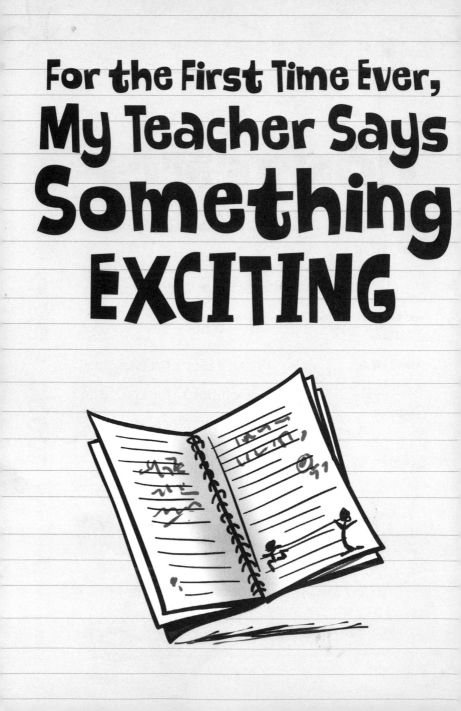

It started as an ordinary day at school. As usual, I doodled in my notebook, looked at the clock every minute, and ignored Mr. McNutty, my teacher.

Then Mr. McNutty loudly cleared his throat. It sounded gross, like he was moving around a bunch of chewed up stuff inside his mouth.

He said, "Now that I have your attention, I have something exciting to tell you."

I groaned. My teacher's idea of something exciting was a lot different than *my* idea of something exciting. Here are some things that he had said were exciting:

- My entire third grade class had to spend a week without TV, video games, and computers.

- The weather was bad, so we had to stay inside at recess.

• It was classroom cleanup day.

Now do you see why I wasn't excited?

I raised my hand and said, "We've already had the excitement of no TV, no recess, and no messy desks. What do we have to give up now? Food? Water? Breathing?"

"Don't be silly," Mr. McNutty said. "You won't be giving up anything. You're *getting* something: a class talent show. Isn't that exciting?"

No one responded. A class talent show was better than a week without TV. But it sure didn't seem exciting.

"The show will be in two weeks. You'll perform in the school auditorium. And it will be in the evening so all of your families can come," Mr. McNutty said.

I ignored him after that, even more than usual. I did not want to go to my school at night. Being in school all day was bad enough.

Rudy Morse asked the teacher, "What's the prize for winning the talent show?"

"There's no prize," Mr. McNutty said.

"No prize? No thanks," I said.

"It is a great opportunity to show your friends and family your talents," the teacher said.

"My friends and family already know what I'm talented at," Rudy said. "Let me remind you."

"I know what you're talented at. Please don't remind me," I said.

"I don't want a reminder, either," Aaron Glass said.

But it was too late. Rudy let out a giant, loud, and extremely smelly fart. "I should get a prize for showing off that talent," he said.

"Your prize for showing off that talent is to stay inside during recess today," Mr. McNutty said. Then he pinched his nostrils and fanned the stinky fart air away from his face.

"My cousin was in a talent show with a huge prize. She could have won half a million dollars," Aaron said.

"Like the winner of that TV show, *America's Next Superstar*?" I asked.

"That's the show my cousin was on. Her name's Brassy Glass."

"Brassy Glass is your cousin?" I asked Aaron. "She was my favorite on that show. That's awesome!"

"Zeke, sit down and stop shouting," Mr. McNutty said.

I hadn't realized I was standing or shouting. I sat down.

Then I asked Aaron, "Can I meet your cousin? Can I get her autograph? Could she sing a song for me?"

"Zeke, you're standing and shouting again," Mr. McNutty said.

Oops. I sat down and closed my mouth.

"Brassy is going to stay with my family in a few weeks. She promised to take us out to dinner. Maybe she can come to the talent show," Aaron said.

"That would be incredible!" I exclaimed.

"Zeke, sit down and stop shouting," my teacher said.

Oops again. I returned to my seat and put my hand over my mouth.

Grace Chang raised her hand. She said, "I don't believe Brassy Glass is Aaron Glass's cousin. Brassy is beautiful, talented, and charming. Aaron is none of those things."

"Yeah. He's none of those things," Emma G. said.

"Yeah. He's none of those things," Emma J. said.

"I am not none of those things. I admit that I'm not beautiful. And I'm not talented. And I'm not charming, either," Aaron said.

Then he scratched his head. "Oh. Maybe I *am* none of those things. But I have something you don't have. I have a famous cousin who's beautiful, talented, and charming."

"That's true," Grace said.

"Yeah. That's true," Emma G. said.

"Yeah. That's true," Emma J. said.

Then the class told Aaron he was lucky, and we talked about who we liked best on *America's Next Superstar* and how much we wanted to meet Brassy Glass.

"Settle down," Mr. McNutty said.

The recess bell rang. No one settled down. Everyone hurried out of their seats and ran outside.

Grace told Aaron, "I don't believe your cousin is Brassy Glass. Prove it. Call her right now. Invite her to our talent show." She handed Aaron her cell phone.

Aaron punched some numbers into the phone. He said, "Hi, Brassy. It's Aaron. Can you come to my class's talent show in two weeks?"

After a minute, Aaron said, "Hold on." Then he told Grace, "My cousin said she'll come to the talent show."

Grace rolled her eyes. "Oh, sure. I bet you're just pretending to talk to Brassy Glass."

"Yeah. You're just pretending," Emma G. said.

"Yeah. You're just pretending," Emma J. said.

Aaron handed the phone to Grace.

"Who is this really? You can't fool me," she said into the phone.

A few seconds later, Grace's mouth opened wide. A few seconds after that, she fell to the ground.

Emma G. and Emma J. fanned Grace with their arms.

Aaron bent over and took the phone from Grace.

He said, "Thanks, Brassy. See you soon."
Then he hung up.

Grace opened her eyes and said, "Oh, wow. That really *was* Brassy Glass. She promised to come to the talent show. She said she'd decide which kid is the most talented. And she'll give that kid personal advice. Oh, wow. Oh, wow. Oh, wow."

Oh, wow! I couldn't wait to be in the talent show! I needed to be the most talented kid in the show so I could get personal advice from Brassy Glass. It was going to be the most exciting night ever!

There was only one little, itsy bitsy, tiny problem: I had no talent.

When I got home from school, I said, "Guess what? Brassy Glass is coming to our class talent show!"

"Stop shouting," my older sister, Alexa, said.

"But it's Brassy Glass!" I shouted.

"Bratty Gas? What's that?" Mom asked.

"It's not a *what*. It's a *she*. Brassy Glass from *America's Next Superstar!* She'll be at our talent show. She's my favorite singer," I said.

"My favorite singer is Princess Sing-Along. If she went on *America's Next Superstar*, she would win," my little sister, Mia, said.

I shook my head. Princess Sing-Along wasn't even real. She was the star of a silly TV show for little kids. She sang annoying songs in a screechy voice.

Mia started singing an annoying Princess Sing-Along song in a screechy voice.

I clamped my hands over my ears.

Our dog, Waggles, clamped his paws over his ears.

But Mia's Princess Sing-Along song came through loud and clear and screechy: "Broccoli can be a drag, la la la. And spinach might make you gag, la la la. But that green stuff keeps you strong, la la la. Even though it tastes so wrong, la la la."

I said, "Brassy Glass is much more talented than Princess Sing-Along."

Mia crossed her arms. "Princess Sing-Along may not be America's Next Superstar. But she *is* America's current superstar."

I rolled my eyes.

"Zeke, are you going to be in the class talent show?" Mom asked.

"Of course I am. I want to thrill Brassy Glass with my talent. Then she'll talk to me after the show and give me personal advice. Brassy Glass seems so nice."

"You used to think Long Legs Carter seemed nice too," Alexa said.

I frowned. Alexa was right. Long Legs Carter had seemed really nice. He was a famous basketball player who could make baskets from just about anywhere on the court. I had hung a poster of him on my bedroom wall. Then he was caught stealing money from a charity. He wasn't nice after all. I threw away my poster of him.

"Everyone makes mistakes about people," I told Alexa. "Remember when those movie stars, Jett Hudd and Lucy Rue, got married? You were sure they'd stay married forever and ever and ever."

Alexa sighed. "Then they broke up after only forty-six days."

"But I think Brassy Glass really *is* nice. On TV, she always smiles and acts sweet. And she's a great singer. I want to meet her so bad," I said. "All I have to do is find a talent."

"Where did you see it last? Did you look under the couch?" Alexa asked.

"Ha, ha." I didn't laugh. I glared at her.

"I know what you could do for the talent show. You could show off pretty dance moves like this," said Mia. She spun around in circles.

Waggles spun around next to her.

Mia got dizzy. She tripped over Waggles.

Both of them fell onto the floor.

I shook my head.

"How about this talent?" Alexa walked slowly across the room, moving her hips from side to side.

"What kind of talent is that?" I asked.

"A talent for modeling clothes, of course," she said.

"Oh. I thought you were just walking weird."

"Maybe you could train Waggles to do some tricks," Mom suggested.

I looked at Waggles. He was still lying on the floor.

"Sit, Waggles," I said.

He lay there. He did not sit. He drooled.

"Maybe he thought you said *spit* instead of *sit*," Mia said.

I shook my head again. "The talent show is two weeks away. That's not enough time to teach Waggles tricks. I would need months to train him. I might need years. It might not even be possible. Waggles is a great pet, but he's not exactly the brainiest dog in the world."

I glanced at him. He was still lying on the floor.

"Actually, he may be the most brainless dog in the world. Sorry, Waggles." I sat next to him and sighed. I couldn't think of one talent I could perform that would make Brassy Glass want to talk to me.

Waggles drooled on my leg. He was very good at drooling. Too bad drooling wasn't a talent.

I wasn't even good at drooling. The only thing I was talented at was being untalented. And a talent for being untalented didn't even make sense.

I had trouble sleeping that night. And it wasn't just because Waggles was hogging the middle of my bed and snoring loudly. I was too worried to sleep. I wanted to talk to Brassy Glass so bad. But I couldn't think of anything I could do at the talent show.

I was good at making fart sounds with my underarms. But if I did that at the talent show, Mr. McNutty would probably make me stay inside at recess. Plus, Brassy Glass probably wouldn't like hearing fart sounds.

Aaron Glass was so lucky. He would get to sit with his cousin Brassy at the talent show and talk to her at his house.

Suddenly, I sat up in bed. I realized something great. I didn't need to win the talent show. I didn't even need to be in the talent show. In order to talk to Brassy Glass, I just needed to hang around Aaron when Brassy was in town.

But I wasn't good friends with Aaron. I wasn't even okay friends with Aaron. I wasn't really even friends with him at all. I had never even been to his house or met anyone in his family. I lay back down in bed.

Then I sat up again. I realized another great thing. There was still time to become good friends with Aaron. I could act really nice to him and play with him at recess and sit with him at lunch. I could give him a present to help make him like me.

I tried to decide what to give Aaron. I
didn't know much about him or what kinds of
things he enjoyed. I stayed awake a long time
thinking about that and listening to Waggles
snore in the middle of my bed.

The next thing I knew, I heard Mom calling,
"Zeke, Zeke, Zeke."

"Get up or you'll be late to school," Mia
said.

Waggles slobbered on me.

I opened my eyes.

Mom and Mia were standing by my bed. Mia sang, "Hey, sleepyhead, la la la. Get out of bed, la la la. Wipe off that drool, la la la. It's time for school, la la la."

I put my pillow over my head.

"I'd better sing another song to wake you up. This time I'll sing louder," Mia said.

"No!" I yelled. I jumped out of bed and got ready for school as fast as I could.

By the time I remembered to get a present for Aaron, I was already out the door.

I told Mom I'd be right back and ran inside the house. I looked around. I still had no idea what to give Aaron to make him want to be friends with me.

Mom honked her car horn.

I grabbed the first thing I saw, stuffed it into my backpack, and ran to the car.

As soon as Mom dropped me off at school, I looked for Aaron

A big crowd of kids stood in front of the building.

What was going on? Were people fighting? Had someone gotten hurt? I rushed over.

Almost everyone in my class was mobbed around Aaron.

Buffy Maynard said, "Aaron, you have pretty eyes."

Nicole Finkle said, "Aaron's eyes aren't just pretty. They're beautiful."

"Who cares about his eyes?" Owen Leach said. "Aaron, you have a great personality. I want to be your best friend."

"Aaron, you should be best friends with me instead. I brought you something," Laurie Schneider said. She handed him a giant chocolate bar.

"I have an even better present for you. You should be my best friend. And you should invite me to your house to meet your cousin," Owen said. He gave Aaron a video game.

"I have the best gift of all," I said. I reached into my backpack and took out what I'd grabbed this morning. I handed it to Aaron.

"A loaf of bread?" he asked.

Everyone started laughing.

Owen pointed to the bread.

He said, "It's only half a loaf. Someone already ate the other half. I bet what's left for Aaron is old and stale."

"The candy bar I gave Aaron is much better than bread. And I didn't eat any of it," Laurie said.

I felt my face flush with embarrassment. I walked away as fast as I could.

Owen called after me, "Goodbye, Bread Boy."

Other kids repeated, "Goodbye, Bread Boy."

My best friend, Hector Cruz, told them to stop calling me that. But they didn't stop.

Owen said, "Aaron, you shouldn't let your cousin Brassy meet Zeke. He might try to give her the other half of the stale loaf of bread."

I sighed sadly. I knew I'd never get invited to Aaron's house now.

I also never wanted to eat bread again.

After being called Bread Boy all day at
school, I was happy to get home.

I was even happier when I opened my front
door. My house smelled like a bakery. I took a
big, long sniff. What a great aroma! I didn't
know what Mom had baked, but I knew I
wanted to eat it.

Mom said, "Hello, Zeke. Have you seen the
bread that was on the kitchen counter this
morning?"

I shrugged and looked away.

"I wanted to make a sandwich. But I couldn't find the bread anywhere," Mom said.

"It was probably just half a loaf, and it was probably stale, too," I said.

Mom stared at me. "Are you sure you haven't seen it?"

"I'm sure," I said. That wasn't exactly a lie. I *was* sure. I was sure I *had* seen the bread. I was sure I gave the bread to Aaron. I was sure I shouldn't have done that. I was sure I would never get invited to Aaron's house now. I was sure my new nickname at school was Bread Boy. And I was sure Mom would be mad if she found out I took the bread.

"Since I couldn't find the bread, I made my own," Mom said. "It took me hours and hours and it was a lot of work."

"It smells wonderful," I said.

"I just took it out of the oven. It will be ready to eat in a few minutes."

Waggles came into the room. He wore a thick pink bow around his neck. Luckily for him, he wasn't smart enough to know how silly he looked.

I bent down and patted him.

He licked my cheek with his big, slobbery tongue. Luckily for him, he wasn't smart enough to know how gross that was.

"Do you like the pretty bow I put on Waggles?" Mia asked.

I shook my head.

Waggles shook his head too.

"Did you think of a talent yet?" Alexa asked.

I shook my head again.

Waggles shook his head again too.

"You could sing a Princess Sing-Along song," Mia said. Then she sang, "Use the potty. Don't forget, la la la. Or you'll make your undies wet, la la la."

I put my hands over my ears.

Waggles put his paws over his ears.

Mia's singing was horrible. I could do better than that.

Hmm. Maybe I could sing at the talent show. I started singing a song I'd heard on the radio: "It's a glorious, gloooriouuuus, gloooooooooriouuuuuuus wooooooooorld." I sang the last few words very slowly and very loudly. "How was that?" I asked.

Mia and Alexa shook their heads.

Waggles shook his head.

"That bad?" I asked.

"Worse," Alexa and Mia said.

Waggles barked.

"I think you should try a different talent," Mom said.

"I think I should eat a snack first. And that snack should be freshly baked bread." I took another big whiff. Mmm.

"The bread just needs a few more minutes to cool," Mom said.

"You could do gymnastics for the talent show," Mia said. She did a cartwheel. It looked easy.

I tried doing a cartwheel. I hurt my back and landed in a heap on the rug.

"How about a handstand?" Alexa suggested. She did a handstand.

I tried it. I twisted my wrist and landed in another heap on the rug.

Alexa and Mia shook their heads again.

Waggles shook his head again too.

I refused to give up. There had to be a talent I could perform. I got an idea. I could juggle. I pictured Brassy Glass clapping for me as I juggled three balls, a sword, a lit torch, and Waggles.

I was getting a little carried away. I didn't know how to juggle and didn't have much time to learn. I might have to settle for juggling two balls and a stick.

I looked around for something to practice with. I didn't see anything. Then I looked down. Aha! I could juggle my shoes.

I took them off and threw one into the air. I caught it easily.

I threw the other one and caught it easily too.

Hey, I was good at this. I bet Brassy Glass would love my juggling act.

I threw both my shoes high into the air.

I caught one.

Then I heard a thud. It came from the kitchen.

"No!" Mom screamed.

I looked over there. Uh-oh. My shoe had landed in the middle of the loaf of Mom's homemade bread.

Mom glared at me and said, "Ezekiel Heathcliff Meeks." She used my full name when she was mad at me. Then she said, "Ezekiel Heathcliff Meeks" again. She used my full name twice when she was doubly mad at me.

"I guess juggling isn't my talent," I said.

"Ezekiel Heathcliff Meeks," Mom said for the third time.

"Sorry. I'll be in my bedroom," I said.

I walked away sadly. The only talent I had was for ruining things.

The next week at school was even worse than usual. Mr. McNutty gave us extra math lessons. So I paid extra less attention. Also, I spent all five days being called Bread Boy about twenty times a day. That added up to being called Bread Boy a lot of times. I didn't know how many times because I didn't pay attention to math lessons.

By the end of the week, I was very worried. Brassy Glass was coming to town soon. I still didn't have a talent. And I knew Aaron Glass wouldn't invite me to his house.

Aaron had turned into a bear. Well, not a real bear. He was still a human being, but he acted as mean as a bear. I wished he *had* turned into a real bear. Then he wouldn't have been able to talk. And he'd have been far away from me, in a forest or a zoo.

At lunchtime on Friday, Owen Leach handed Aaron his lunchbox. Owen had done that all week.

Aaron opened the lunchbox and took out Owen's chocolate chip cookies and his carton of fruit punch. Then he threw the lunchbox back to Owen. He said, "You can keep the turkey sandwich and carrots for yourself. Tell your mom to pack more junk food and less healthy stuff."

"Can I come to your house when your cousin is there?" Owen asked him.

Aaron sneered. "You've been asking me that every day. I still haven't decided. On Monday, bring me two vanilla cupcakes with chocolate frosting and rainbow sprinkles, a large bag of barbeque potato chips, and a carton of strawberry lemonade."

"But my mom won't let me —"

Aaron interrupted Owen. "I don't care about your mom. If you want to meet my cousin Brassy, you'd better give me what I want."

Owen nodded and walked away.

Danny Ford came by and said, "Hi, Aaron."

"That's not what you're supposed to call me," Aaron said.

"Oh, yeah. Hi, Awesome Aaron."

Aaron smiled.

"Do you want me to do your homework again, Awesome Aaron?" Danny asked.

"Of course. And make sure you write neatly," Aaron said.

"Will you please let me meet your cousin?" Danny asked.

Aaron shrugged. "I'm still deciding. Do a good job on my homework."

Now do you see what I mean about Aaron acting like a bear? He wasn't awesome. He was awful.

Behind his back, people called him Awful Aaron. But it was still a better nickname than Bread Boy.

At least no one called me Bread Boy at home. But things weren't going well for me there, either. I had tried all kinds of things, but I wasn't talented at any of them.

After school that day, I performed a magic show for Mia. I gave her a cloth napkin and said, "Look at it closely. Then hand it back to me."

She stared at the napkin and asked, "Is it going to turn into a real, live bird? I saw someone do that on *America's Next Superstar*."

"No. The napkin isn't going to turn into a bird," I said.

"A real, live rabbit?"

"Not a rabbit, either. I can't turn a napkin into a live animal. I'm just a kid," I said.

Mia sneezed. Then she wiped her nose with the napkin and gave it back to me.

"You weren't supposed to get snot on it," I said.

"Princess Sing-Along says it's okay to get snot on napkins," she said. Then she started singing: "A sleeve, a chair, and a cot, la la la, are bad places to put snot, la la la. Napkins and tissues are fine, la la la, for wiping your booger slime, la la la."

I shook my head. "I don't care what Princess Sing-Along says. It's not fine to put your boogers on my napkin."

"Do you want me to watch your magic trick or not?" she asked.

I sighed. "I do." I put the disgusting napkin in my pocket.

"Is that the trick? Putting a napkin in your pocket? It looks like you had a lot of stuff in your pocket already. I bet it was hard to get the napkin in there," Mia said.

"Just watch," I said. I pulled a napkin out of my pocket. It was tied to another cloth napkin. That napkin was tied to another napkin. And that napkin was tied to another one.

I held up my chain of napkins. Then I bowed.

Next to me, Waggles bowed.

Mia yawned.

Waggles yawned.

"Isn't that trick amazing?" I asked.

Mia shook her head.

Waggles shook his head.

"Why was your pocket so full before I gave you the napkin back? Did you already have napkins tied up in your pocket?" Mia asked.

I frowned. "Maybe magic isn't my best talent. I'll put on a different show for you."

I got out two puppets that I had made from lunch bags. Then I asked Mia, "Would you like to see a puppet show?"

"I love puppet shows!" she exclaimed.

I put my paper bag puppets on top of the
coffee table. I crouched behind the table and
made my puppets say silly things and move
around. I thought I put on a great show. I
might have finally found my talent: puppeteer.

At the end of the show, my puppets said,
"The end," and bowed low.

I waited for Mia to clap.

But she didn't clap. She didn't make a sound.

"Did you love my show?" I asked.

She didn't answer.

"Did you *like* my show?" I asked.

She still didn't answer.

I got up from behind the coffee table and looked at Mia.

She was asleep.

Next to her, Waggles was asleep too. Even he didn't like my show.

I'd tried singing, gymnastics, juggling, magic, and puppetry. I'd failed at every one of them. I wasn't talented at anything. There was no way I could be in the talent show. I sighed loudly.

That woke up Waggles. He sighed loudly too.

I shook my head.

Waggles shook his head too.

That gave me an idea. Waggles couldn't learn tricks such as *sit* or *stay* or *beg*, but he liked to copy people.

I could use that for a talent show act. It might be a big success. I pumped my fist in the air.

Waggles pumped his paw in the air.

I sure hoped Brassy Glass liked dogs.

She would probably love Waggles.

I sure did.

Fantastic Zeke and Dorky Dog

Prepare to be amazed by our awesomeness!

The talent show was only a few hours away. Waggles and I had worked hard on our act. I called it Fantastic Zeke and Burly Dog. I thought it was good.

We would look good too, as long as Waggles didn't slobber too much. I had given him a bath and brushed his thick, brown fur last night.

When I came home from school, Alexa greeted me at the door. She said, "I know this talent show is important to you. So I made Waggles look like a star." She called him over.

My mouth dropped open when I saw Waggles.

Alexa grinned. "You're speechless. You must really love what I did with our dog. It's okay. You can thank me later."

I was speechless because I was in shock. Alexa had dyed Waggles's fur bright pink. He no longer looked like a burly dog. He looked like a dorky dog. It wasn't okay at all.

"I also bought Waggles a purple sweater with pink sequins. It will look nice with his pink fur. Don't you agree?" Alexa said.

I was still in shock. I shook my head and said, "Urg," "Bleh," and "Oof." I could no longer call our act Fantastic Zeke and Burly Dog. I changed the name to Fantastic Zeke and Dorky Dog.

I spent a few more hours in shock. But I was okay by the time my family and I got to the school auditorium.

We were early. I hoped Brassy Glass would arrive before the talent show started. I really wanted to meet her. Her cousin Aaron had gotten lots of attention and free food and homework help.

But he hadn't let anyone from our class meet Brassy.

I kept watching the door of the auditorium, hoping to see Brassy walk in. She was so pretty and sweet on TV. I bet she was even prettier and sweeter in person.

Waggles watched the door too. He wagged his pink tail and drooled all over his seat. That meant he was happy. He must not have known how dorky he looked.

Hector walked in and sat next to me.

I said, "I'm glad to see you. But I can't wait to see Brassy Glass. She's one of my biggest heroes."

Hector raised his eyebrows. "Really? My heroes are Abraham Lincoln, who helped end slavery, and firefighters, who rescue people from burning buildings. What heroic thing has Brassy Glass done?"

I shrugged. "She made it to the top ten in *America's Next Superstar*. And she seems nice."

Hector nodded.

But I wondered whether Brassy should really be one of my biggest heroes. When I compared her to Abraham Lincoln and firefighters, she didn't seem very heroic.

Aaron Glass came in with his parents. Behind them, Brassy Glass finally entered the auditorium. She looked different tonight. Her eyes seemed smaller, like little beads. Her eyebrows were scrunched together. Her lips turned down in the shape of a dead, dried out worm.

I wondered why she looked so much worse tonight than she did on TV. I stared at her some more and realized why: She was scowling.

I still really wanted to meet her. I walked toward her. A bunch of other people did too.

"Stop," Brassy said loudly. "I'm here only as a favor to Aaron's family. They're letting me stay with them so I don't have to pay for a hotel. I'll talk to one lucky kid after the show, but that's it. Now leave me alone, unless you want my autograph or a picture with me."

I wanted an autograph and a picture. I started moving toward Brassy again.

"I charge ten dollars for each autograph and twenty dollars for a picture," she said.

Everyone backed away.

Laurie Schneider asked, "Could you sing a song for us, Brassy?"

"Yes. I charge two hundred dollars per song," Brassy said.

"That's a lot of money. You weren't even in the final four of *America's Next Superstar*," I said.

"Don't talk to me," she said.

I hurried back to my seat. I had been wrong. Brassy Glass wasn't as pretty or as nice as she seemed on TV. In fact, her scowl made her look sort of ugly. And she seemed sort of mean.

Brassy took a seat right behind me. Then she pointed at Waggles and said, "Mangy dogs aren't allowed at school."

I didn't know what the word *mangy* meant. But the way Brassy said it, I was pretty sure it wasn't a kind word. I said, "My teacher told me I could bring my dog tonight. And he's not mangy."

Brassy scowled even harder. "*He?* A boy dog with pink fur? I hope that mangy thing isn't in the talent show."

Waggles whimpered.

I patted him on his pink head and said, "Don't let Brassy Glass scare you. You'll be the best thing about the show."

He put his paws over his face.

"Do you have stage fright? Or do you have Brassy fright? Or both?" I asked.

Waggles started trembling.

If he was shaking with fear now, how could he be brave enough to perform onstage? I'd have to change the name of our act to Fantastic Zeke and Scared Dog. We'd probably get booed.

Just thinking about that made me shake a little too.

Nasty Noises, Harmed HAIRPIECES, and Sudden SLEEPINESS

Mr. McNutty walked onstage and said, "Welcome, everyone. We have a terrific show tonight."

I whispered to Waggles, "Did you hear my teacher? It's supposed to be a terrific show. Cheer up."

But Waggles kept his head under his paws.

Owen Leach was the first performer. He walked onstage with a violin.

"Violins are my favorite instrument. They make such pretty music," Mom said.

Owen started playing. He did not make pretty music. The sounds he made couldn't really be called music. They were more like a mixture of fighting cats, squealing brakes, and crying babies.

Mom whispered, "I guess violins don't always make pretty music."

I whispered to Waggles, "Our act is better than that."

But I wasn't sure about that anymore. Waggles was still trembling.

Brassy Glass pointed to Owen and said, "If he played the violin like that on *America's Next Superstar*, he'd be kicked off the show."

If Mr. McNutty heard Brassy talk like that, she'd be kicked out of the auditorium.

Laurie Schneider came onstage next. She wore a ballet leotard, tutu, and tights. They were the same bright shade of pink as Waggles's dyed fur. "My talent is ballet dancing," she said. She ran across the stage, kicking her legs.

One of her feet got tangled in the stage curtain. She almost fell on her face.

"This is the worst show ever," Brassy said.

Brassy seemed like the worst person ever.

Laurie got up and twirled in circles at the front of the stage. She looked as if she was about to fall off the stage.

"Watch out!" Mr. McNutty called. He rushed over and grabbed her before she could get hurt.

"Thanks for catching me, Mr. McNutty," Laurie said. She did another twirl, jumped in the air, and flung out her arms.

Her left arm hit Mr. McNutty's head, knocking his hairpiece to the ground.

"Oops. Sorry," Laurie said. She ran off the stage.

She got a big round of applause from all the kids.

Mr. McNutty did not applaud. He
quickly returned his hairpiece to his head.
Unfortunately, he put it on sideways. It was not
a good look for him. But to be fair, a sideways
hairpiece wouldn't be a good look for anyone.

I patted Waggles and said, "That was funny.
But our act will be better."

Waggles whimpered again.

Mr. McNutty said, "The next act calls herself Victoria Crow, the Smartest Kid in Third Grade."

Victoria Crow really was the smartest kid in third grade. But I didn't know if she had any talent besides being smart.

She said, "I am the smartest kid in third grade. I will now recite a poem called *Beowulf*. It's 3,182 lines long and about a thousand years old. I have memorized all of it." Then she started reciting the poem.

I realized what Victoria's talent was: being boring. She was great at it. Her poetry reading was more boring than math homework. It was more boring than a long car ride. It was more boring than Mom's talk radio. Her poetry reading was even more boring than doing math homework on a long car ride while listening to Mom's talk radio.

Victoria's act was so boring that Mia fell asleep in one minute.

A minute after that, Alexa fell asleep, too.

I wasn't sure what happened after that, because I fell asleep.

I woke up when Mr. McNutty shouted, "That's enough, Victoria! You can't recite all 3,182 lines of that poem. Stop. Please, please, please stop!"

Victoria stopped.

The people who were awake clapped loudly.

"Did you get a nice nap, Waggles?" I asked.

Waggles was still trembling.

Mr. McNutty said, "The next act is Fantastic Zeke and Dorky Dog."

Brassy said, "I can't stand dogs. They're almost as annoying as kids."

I stood up and said, "Come on, Waggles. We'll show Brassy how great dogs and kids can be. Let's do the act we've been practicing all week."

But Waggles stayed in his seat, still shaking with fear.

Suspenders, RUBBISH, AND Cinderella

What do these things
have in common?
You'll find out. Maybe.

"Mr. McNutty, my dog isn't ready to go onstage yet. Could we have a few more minutes?" I asked.

"But I told everyone the order of the acts a few days ago. It's not fair to the other performers," he said.

Hector Cruz stood up and said, "I'll go onstage now. It's no problem."

I gave him a smile. He was a great best friend.

"All right," Mr. McNutty said. "Everyone please welcome Hilarious Hector."

I clapped hard as Hector walked onstage to do his comedy act.

Hector looked down at his clothes and said, "I was going to wear my suspenders tonight, but they're in jail. They were in a holdup."

Some people laughed. Brassy said, "That wasn't very funny."

I turned around and shushed her.

Then Hector said, "I'm worried about my pet pig. He hurt himself today. I had to call a hambulance."

Almost everyone laughed at that joke. Even Waggles perked up a little.

Hector said, "I won't tell you the joke about the garbage truck. It's rubbish."

That got even more laughter. Hector was really good. Waggles sat up in his chair.

"I had a test today, so I brought scissors to school." Hector said. "I wanted to cut class."

Everyone around me laughed. Waggles gave a happy little "arf."

Hector added, "The scissors didn't help. But my teacher said the test was a piece of cake. So I ate it."

I was laughing so much it was hard to breathe. Mom was snorting with glee. Even Mr. McNutty was bent over in laughter. Waggles wagged his tail.

"At recess, I played soccer with Cinderella," Hector said. "She wasn't very good at it. She ran away from the ball."

The laughter got even louder.

Hector took a bow and left the stage. People were still laughing and clapping. Hector really was hilarious. I was proud of my best friend.

Waggles kept wagging his tail. The jokes and laughter had cheered him up. Maybe he was finally ready to perform with me.

9

Mr. McNutty returned to the stage. "That was very funny. But please don't bring scissors to school or eat my tests," he said. Then he looked at me and asked, "Are you and your dog ready now, Zeke?"

I glanced at Waggles. He was still wagging his tail.

"We're ready," I said.

Mr. McNutty smiled. "Our next act is hopefully worth waiting for. Please clap for Fantastic Zeke and Dorky Dog."

I stood up and walked to the front of the auditorium. Waggles and Mia followed me, just as we'd planned.

We quickly got onstage. I said, "To start our act, my sister will sing a song from the *Princess Sing-Along* TV show."

Mia started singing: "Take your dog for lots of walks, la la la. Let him play with grass and rocks, la la la. But scoop up his stinky dog doo, la la la, before it gets on someone's shoe, la la la."

While she sang, I moved to the side of the stage. I put my hands over my ears.

That made Waggles put his paws over his ears.

Everyone laughed.

When Waggles looked at me, I shook my head.

I returned to the center of the stage and said, "Should we let Mia sing another Princess Sing-Along song?"

Waggles copied what I'd just done. He shook his head.

Everyone laughed again.

"Sorry, Mia. No more singing for you," I said. She left the stage, and everyone clapped.

I stood in front of Waggles. I had my back to the audience so they couldn't see what I was doing. I said, "Waggles, what have you heard about our school?" Then I yawned.

Waggles yawned too.

"Yeah, it's pretty boring," I said.

I heard a lot of laughter.

"Waggles, my sister Alexa dyed your fur today. How do you like your new pink fur?" I asked. I shook my head slightly.

Waggles shook his head too.

"What would you like to do to Alexa?" I asked. With my back to the audience, I punched the air with my fist.

Waggles punched the air with his paw.

We got more laughs.

I turned around and said, "Well, Waggles, I guess you're not so dorky after all. Let's take a bow."

I bowed.

Then Waggles bowed.

Everyone clapped loudly for us.

After we walked back to our seats, Mia said, "Waggles did a great job pretending he didn't like my song."

I didn't tell Mia that he wasn't pretending.

Brassy tapped me on the shoulder and said, "You and your mangy dog weren't bad."

I shrugged. "Thanks, but Waggles isn't mangy. Whatever that means."

The last act was called "Chandler Fitzgerald, the Great Actor." I didn't know Chandler liked to act. All I knew about him was that he was in my class and that he cried a lot.

Chandler said, "First, I will act like a cat who can't find his toy." He said, "Meow." Then he started to cry.

Everyone clapped.

"Now I will pretend to be a boy who just broke his leg." Chandler sat on the ground, said "Ow," and started to cry.

Most people in the audience clapped.

"Now I will act like a bird with a broken wing." Chandler bent his arm and moved his elbow up and down. Then he cried again.

About half the audience clapped.

Behind me, Brassy said, "That isn't acting. That's just crying."

"Now I will pretend to be a pebble that's been stepped on." Chandler sat onstage and cried again.

A few people clapped.

Brassy called out, "Pebbles are just little rocks. They don't cry."

"Yes they do. Pebbles have soft, tiny cries. They're so small you can't hear them. You hurt my feelings." Chandler started crying again.

"Who are you pretending to be now?" Mr. McNutty asked.

"I'm not pretending. I'm just being myself, a boy who cries a lot."

Mr. McNutty patted Chandler's head. Then he said, "Let's all clap for Chandler Fitzgerald, the Great Actor." He gave Chandler a tissue. Then he helped him off the stage.

Mr. McNutty said, "That ends the talent portion of our show. I think the kids did a great job."

Everyone clapped.

"Now let me introduce a special guest here tonight with Aaron Glass. She's a wonderful singer. She made it to the top ten on the TV show *America's Next Superstar*. Please give a big hand to Brassy Glass."

Brassy started walking toward the stage.

Mr. McNutty clapped. So did a few other people. Most people did not clap.

I crossed my arms.

Waggles whimpered.

Mr. McNutty said, "Brassy is going to spend a few minutes with the performer she thinks had the best act tonight."

Brassy stood onstage and blew kisses to the audience.

Yuck.

She said, "Your little show wasn't as bad as I expected. Of course, no one is as talented as me. But there was one act I liked the best. And that act is . . ." She didn't say anything.

"Are you all right?" Mr. McNutty asked.

She nodded. "I'm just pausing for the sake of suspense. They do that on *America's Next Superstar.*"

Mr. McNutty looked at his watch.

"I should make everyone wait for my decision until after the commercials," Brassy said.

"There are no commercials tonight. This isn't a TV show. It's just a school talent show," Mr. McNutty said.

"But I want everyone to eagerly wait for my decision and watch me breathlessly."

I rolled my eyes.

Waggles rolled his eyes.

"Let's just get on with it. We're tired of waiting," Mr. McNutty said.

He was right. Some people were standing up and getting ready to leave.

"No one here is as talented as me," Brassy Glass said.

"You said that already," Laurie Schneider's mother called out.

"You have a talent for being irritating," Owen Leach's father said.

Mr. McNutty said, "Everyone please be quiet."

"Yes. Be quiet so you can hear me speak," Brassy said. "Here is my decision . . ."

Then she paused again.

Brassy Glass was getting on my nerves. I wished she'd hurry up and announce which act she liked best. I didn't really care about her decision anymore. I just wanted her to get off the stage.

"Even though I don't like dogs, the mangy dog named Waggles did a pretty god job tonight," Brassy said. "So I will give personal advice to his owner, Zeke."

"Nice job, Zeke. Your hero liked your act," Hector said.

Mom patted me on the shoulder and said, "Good going, Zeke. You got what you wanted."

I was proud of myself and proud of Waggles. I'd wanted to have a good act for the show. Waggles and I had worked hard. And we had done well. Mom was right. I had gotten what I'd wanted: the chance to talk to my hero.

But Brassy Glass didn't seem like a hero anymore. And I didn't want to talk to her anymore.

I stood up and said, "Thank you, Brassy. But I have made a decision of my own. I don't want your personal advice." If I followed her advice, I could become as mean as her. No thanks.

"You're turning me down? What a fool," Brassy said.

Waggles barked at her.

People started walking out of the auditorium.

Brassy said, "Don't leave. I'll choose someone else."

I looked around. Almost everyone was leaving.

Brassy said, "My second place pick is Hilarious Hector. But I wouldn't call him hilarious. Most of his jokes weren't very funny."

Hector shook his head. "I don't want to meet with you. Thanks anyway."

"Doesn't anyone want my personal advice?" Brassy asked.

Mia stood up and shouted, "I do! I'm a singer just like you. Could you listen to my songs and give me personal advice?"

Brassy smiled. "All right."

"Get ready to cover your ears again," I told Waggles.

Mia rushed onstage and said, "*America's Next Superstar* is an okay TV show. But I like *Princess Sing-Along* much better. Here are a few songs from the show."

She screeched, "Don't pet a dog you don't know, la la la. Even if it wears a bow, la la la. It may want to start a fight, la la la, that ends in a bloody bite, la la la." She took a deep breath and asked, "How was my singing?"

Brassy frowned. "It was —"

Mia interrupted her. "It was wonderful. I know. I have a great voice. Here's another song. Tell me which one you like better." She started singing again: "Make sure you eat protein, la la la. Like chicken, fish, and beans, la la la. But you should take this to heart, la la la. Too many beans make you fart, la la la." She asked Brassy, "What did you think of that?"

Before Brassy could answer, Mia sang another song: "Make sure to treat your body well, la la la. Take nightly baths so you won't smell, la la la. Brush your teeth and brush your hair, la la la. Don't wear dirty underwear, la la la."

"Stop!" Brassy yelled.

"I was just getting started. I know a lot more songs. I could sing them to you all night long," Mia said.

Brassy started running out of the auditorium.

Aaron Glass was running out of there too.

Owen and Danny ran after him.

"Aaron, stop!" Owen shouted. "You didn't tell us your cousin Brassy was so mean. You'd better bring me lunch every day next week!"

"And you'd better do all my homework next week, Awful Aaron!" Danny shouted.

Mom patted my head. She said, "You did a great job at the talent show. Too bad Brassy Glass turned out to be a lot different than she seemed on TV."

"At least I learned a lesson," I said.

"Not to believe everything you see on TV about celebrities?" she asked.

I shrugged. "I was thinking of a different lesson, on how to make mean people suffer: Have Mia sing them Princess Sing-Along songs."

Mia yelled, "Wait, Brassy! I want to sing the Princess Sing-Along song about vomit."

I put my hands over my ears. Waggles put his paws over his ears.

But I was smiling and he was wagging his tail.

ABOUT THE AUTHOR

D. L. Green lives in California with her husband, three children, silly dog, and a big collection of rubber chickens. She loves to read, write, and joke around.

ABOUT THE ILLUSTRATOR

Josh Alves's last talent show experience taught him how difficult it is to juggle with a spotlight shining in your eyes. Josh gets to juggle, draw, and play his guitar in his studio in Maine where he lives with his wonderful wife and their three awesome kids.

IS THERE ANYTHING WORSE THAN BEING IN A TALENT SHOW?

(And other really important questions)

Write answers to these questions, or discuss them with your friends and classmates.

1. Is there anything worse than being in a talent show? Well, bugs are worse . . . but anything else?

2. If you had to perform in a talent act, what would you do?

3. Were you surprised that Brassy Glass was so mean? Why or why not?

4. What famous people do you like? How would you feel if you found out that they were awful people?

ANNOYING: Things that are annoying bug you so much you think you might lose it!

APPLAUD: Clap super loud after you see something amazing, like my dog act.

AROMA: A wonderful smell, like fresh bread, but unlike Rudy's farts.

AUDITORIUM: A large room in our school where we had our awful talent show.

BRAINIEST: Smartest, like Victoria Crow.

DISGUSTING: Things that make you go "EW!" like love notes, most girls, and liver.

EMBARRASSMENT: The feeling you have after you do something dumb and people notice and call you awful names like Bread Boy.

EXTREMELY: Super duper, very much so.

FANTASTIC: Super duper great! Better than ever! You've never seen anyting so good. (You get the idea.)

GLORIOUS: Wonderful! (See also, fantastic.)

HILARIOUS: So funny that you laugh and laugh, and maybe almost pee your pants.

Owen's violin playing is screechy. It's also irritating and annoying.

INCREDIBLE: If something is incredible, it is so great you cannot believe your own eyes.

IRRITATING: This is just another word for "annoying." Princess Sing-Along is the perfect example of irritating.

MEMORIZED: Got something in your head so well, you didn't have to look at a paper to know it.

OPPORTUNITY: A chance to do something. Parents are really big on not missing good opportunities.

ORDINARY: Normal, which can sometimes be boring, but not always.

PERSONAL ADVICE: Special tips to help out a certain person.

PERSONALITY: How you think and act makes up your personality. You can have a good personality, like me, or a bad one, like Brassy Glass.

SCOWLED: Frowned with your whole face.

SCREECHY: Loud and high-pitched and awful!

SCRUNCHED: Squeezed something, like your face, all up together really tight!

SNEERED: Said something in a really rude way.

TREMBLING: Shaking because you are so scared, like when you see a beetle!

WHIMPERED: Sighed, whined, and made other sad noises.

Banana Ninja

It could happen to you: You could be asked to be in a talent show. This magic trick might be just the thing you need to steal the show! With an ultra-secret ninja move, you'll slice the banana while it is still in the peel!

What you need:

- banana
- straight pin, like you use in sewing

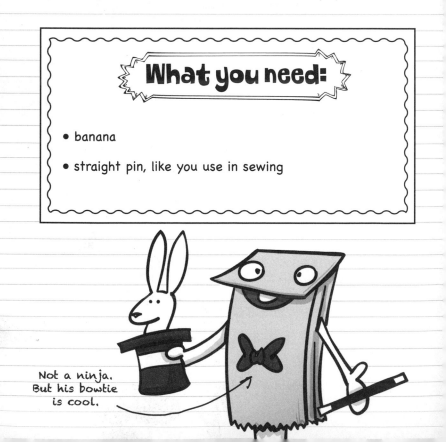

Not a ninja. But his bowtie is cool.

What you do:

1. Before your act, stick the straight pin into the banana where you want it to break. Carefully, move it horizontally to slice the banana inside into separate pieces. Do NOT damage the peel.

2. If you would like several slices, repeat step 1 a few more times.

3. During your act, show the banana to the audience. Then make a big deal about performing a ninja move on the banana. Here is where good acting is important.

4. Slowly unpeel the banana, and show everyone how it has magically sliced inside the peel. They will be amazed! And then you can offer them a piece of banana for a snack, making your act very memorable.

WE ARE
AWESOME
BANANA
NINJAS!

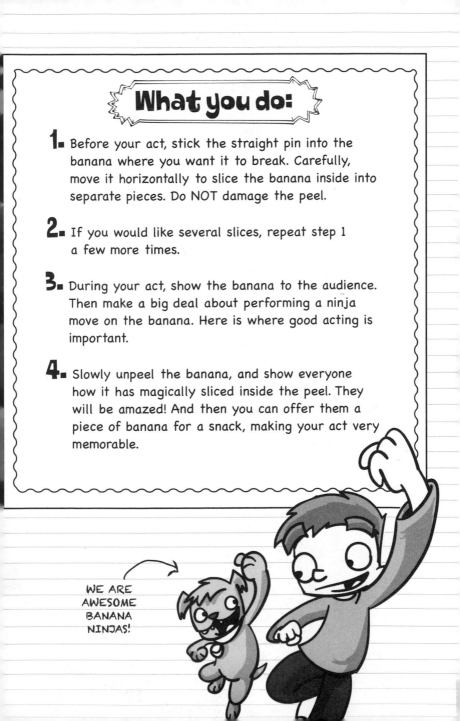

AWESOME HAIR

CHARMING SMILE

COOLEST THIR
GRADER YOU'
EVER MEET!

WWW.CAPSTONEKIDS.COM